THE LITTLEST YAK
THE NEW ARRIVAL

For the real Granny Hilda,
whose heart was endless,
& for wonderful Grannies
everywhere . . . LF xxx

Sincere thanks to the Squires
and Bull Pun Consultancy – KH

SIMON & SCHUSTER
First published in Great Britain in 2022 by
Simon & Schuster UK Ltd 1st Floor, 222 Gray's Inn Road, London WC1X 8HB

Text copyright © 2022 Sarah Louise Maclean • Illustrations copyright © 2022 Kate Hindley

The right of Sarah Louise Maclean and Kate Hindley to be identified as the author and illustrator of
this work has been asserted by them in accordance with the Copyright, Designs and Patents Act, 1988

A CIP catalogue record for this book is available from the British Library upon request

ISBN: 978-1-4711-8263-1 (HB) • ISBN: 978-1-4711-8265-5 (PB) • ISBN: 978-1-4711-8264-8 (eBook)

1 2 3 4 5 6 7 8 9 10 • Printed in Italy

FSC
www.fsc.org
MIX
Paper from
responsible sources
FSC® C023419

THE LITTLEST YAK
THE NEW ARRIVAL

LU FRASER   KATE HINDLEY

SIMON & SCHUSTER
London New York Sydney Toronto New Delhi

On the pointiest peak of a craggy cliff top,

Where the icicles swing and the snow doesn't stop,

There's a mummy yak, under a moon shining brightly

With Gertie, the littlest yak, cuddled tightly . . .

"Oh, I've treasured the time
that's been just you and me,
But soon," Mummy whispered,
"our TWO becomes THREE!"

"We're having a BABY?"
gasped Gertie. "Brand new?

Then I'll be a BIG SISTER GERTIE soon, too!"

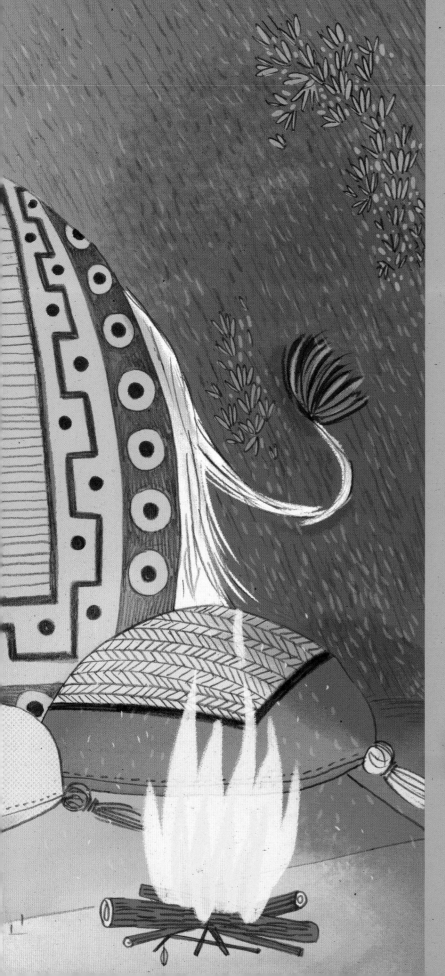

And she dreamed woolly
dreams of sweet yaklings
all night,

'Til BIG SISTER planning
began at first light . . .

"I'll paint a big banner with glittery pens
That says:

HELLO YAKLING!
I HOPE WE'LL BE FRIENDS

And I've heard," Gertie frowned,
"that babies are sticky,
So I'm knitting a bib
(but hooves make it tricky!)."

"Well, in the swish of a tail," Mummy smiled, "I'll be back,
Home to the herd with our new baby yak,

But in case you need hugging, whilst I'm away,
Here's Granny Hilda! She's coming to stay!"

Then they waved a big wave as Mum left, slow but steady
And Gertie showed Gran she was BIG SISTER READY!
"Well, Gertie," Gran nodded, "what *brilliant* preparing,

But what yaklings need *most* is some BIG SISTER sharing!"

"SHARING?!" frowned Gertie and stopped in her tracks.

"Then I'll be the BEST SHARER of *all* sister yaks!"

"Here's my curly-wool comb
for important back-scratching,

My pinecones for playing
yak throwing and catching.

And books full of pictures to help small thoughts grow

Because yaklings have SO much

to learn and to know . . . "

Hmmm, Gertie thought,
is there something I've missed?
What else should I share
on my big sister list?

Then a worrying wobble stirred
deep in her tummy.

"Oh no!" Gertie gulped.
"Will I have to share . . .

. . . MUMMY?!

And . . . OH!" Gertie gasped. "There's an even WORSE part!
Will there be enough space for TWO yaks in her heart?"

"Oh, there's space for a Gertie,"
smiled Gran, looking wise.
"No matter your bigness,
or smallness or size."

But as soon as snores drifted from Granny Yak's head,

On the tip of her hooves,
Gertie slipped from her bed

And she drew Mummy's heart with
her hoof in the snow,

Just to check there was space
for a Gertie to go . . .

Then she piled up the sharing things, all in a stack.

"But there's only room left," Gertie cried, "for . . .

. . . ONE yak!

How will my Mummy
fit BOTH of us in?"
And her woolly face wobbled
from horn-tips to chin.

YAK IN BOOTS

DICK WHITTINGTON
AND HIS YAK

POM-POMS

YAK AND THE BEANSTALK

YAK BEAUTY

"Oh, what do I do?" Gertie whispered, heart sinking.

"This is the TRICKIEST big sister thinking!"

"I need some help to UN-worry my tummy
And my best-of-all fixer of wobbles is . . . MUMMY!
Yes, I'll follow her tracks from our mountainside home."

So, BIG SISTER BRAVE, she set off on her own.

Over the boulders with
springs in her knees,

Then into the forest
of shadow-filled trees . . .

'Til deeper . . .

and darker . . .

and further she stumbled,

A lost little yak
as the snowy flakes tumbled.

But wait!

What was that?

Something was racing . . .

. . . A hundred yak hoofbeats were worriedly chasing.

And leading the herd, with her hooves flying fast,
Was Mummy Yak grunting,
"OH, GERTIE! AT LAST!"

"Mummy!" cried Gertie. "Do you think there might be some space in your heart for a yakling . . .

AND me?"

"Oh, there's *always* a space," Mummy murmured, "for you!"
And she hugged her the way only mummy yaks do.

Then hoof held in hoof,
home they sped with a

WHOOSH!

'Til they stopped at the
higgledy heart with a

SWOOSH!

Where, under the sparkling stars high above,

Mummy knelt and she rubbed out the edges of love.

Then she drew it more HUGELY in powder-puff snow.

"The thing about hearts," Mummy smiled, "is . . . they GROW!"

And she took Gertie's hoof as they stepped in together.

"See, there's room in my heart for you now . . . and *forever.*"

"And, look!" Mummy pointed her hoof high above.
"A new yakling heart to add even MORE love!"
For rocked in a pouch across Mummy Yak's back,
Blinked the woolliest wisp of the mini-est yak!

"Oh, I think," Gertie whispered,
"my heart has stretched, too!
It's grown a bit bigger to make space for . . .

you!"

And there, in the hug of the herd, cuddled tight,
"Our yakling," smiled Gertie,
"is new but . . . all right!

And 'though our herd's grown
and it's changed from before,
I'm not loved any less but . . ."

"... a whole heartful MORE!"